E TUCKER    Tucker, Kathy.

Do knights take
naps?

$15.95

| DATE | | | |
|---|---|---|---|
|  |  |  |  |
|  |  |  |  |
|  |  |  |  |
|  |  |  |  |
|  |  |  |  |
|  |  |  |  |
|  |  |  |  |
|  |  |  |  |
|  |  |  |  |
|  |  |  |  |
|  |  |  |  |
|  |  |  |  |
|  |  |  |  |

# Do Knights Take Naps?

Written by Kathy Tucker
Illustrated by Nick Sharratt

Albert Whitman & Company
Morton Grove, Illinois

Library of Congress Cataloging-in-Publication Data
Tucker, Kathy
Do knights take naps? / by Kathy Tucker ; illustrated by Nick Sharratt.
p. cm.
Summary: Rhyming text explores what it means to be a knight,
what he wears, and what he does for fun.
ISBN 0-8075-1695-3
[1. Knights and knighthood Fiction. 2. Stories in rhyme.]
I. Sharratt, Nick, ill. II. Title.
PZ8.3.T793Di 2000
[E]—dc21 99-35748
CIP

Text copyright © 2000 by Kathleen Tucker Brooks.
Illustrations copyright © 2000 by Nick Sharratt.
Published in 2000 by Albert Whitman & Company,
6340 Oakton Street, Morton Grove, Illinois 60053-2723.
Published simultaneously in Canada by General Publishing, Limited, Toronto.
Printed in the United States of America.
10 9 8 7 6 5 4 3 2 1

# What does a knight do?

He gets up before breakfast
and travels far,
looking for folks to save.
He fights the Bad Prince
and the Fiery Dragon,
who lives in the cool, dark cave.

BAD PRINCE'S
CASTLE
5 MILES

FIERY DRAGON'S
CAVE
7 MILES

# What does a knight wear?

Bright shiny armor
that clinks and clanks
and covers him head to toe.
He lifts his visor
and peeks around
to see which way to go.

# What else does a knight need?

His very own shield,
a swishing sword,
a lance quite skinny and long;
he has a flail
with a ball and chain,
and a horse who's smart and strong.

# How do you get to be a knight?

If you can wrestle
and ride a horse,
if you know what's wrong and right,
you wash your face,
then kneel by the King,
who says, "I dub thee Knight!"

# Where do knights live?

They live in a castle
with towers upstairs
and secret rooms inside.
A creaky drawbridge
goes up and down
o'er a moat dug deep and wide.

# Do knights eat candy?

No candy at all,
just old apple juice
with hunks of salty meat;
some chewy bread,
and if you're good,
there's honey, for a treat.

HONEY

# What does the Bad Prince do?

To capture the castle,
he swims the moat
and tries to scale the wall.
His men throw rocks
with a catapult
and fire a cannonball!

# How do the knights beat the Bad Prince?

They flash their swords
as fast as a blink
and chase the cowardly bunch.
That old Bad Prince
and his creepy men
run back home for lunch!

# What does the Fiery Dragon do?

He roams the country
breathing flames,
giving folks a terrible scare.
He captures a boy
and his *puppy*, too,
roaring, "Catch me if thou dare!"

# How does the knight fight the dragon?

He grabs a bucket
and calls to the beast,
"Come forth, thou nasty bloke!"
He tosses the water –
the dragon's breath
turns into a cloud of smoke!

# Do knights have TV?

They don't have TV,
but they have a court jester,
a guy who tells stories for fun.
He knows how to throw
ten balls in the air
and catch them, every last one.

# What happens at a joust?

While everyone cheers,
knights aim their lances
and ride their horses *fast*.
They try to knock
each other off
(the guy who falls is last).

# What happens if a knight gets hurt?

He doesn't cry
if his knee is skinned
or he has a stomachache.
He fixes the owie,
drinks lots of juice,
then takes a little break.

# Do knights take naps?

Right after lunch
their moms tuck them in
and leave the light on in the hall.
They dream of being
brave and good—
the very best knights of all!

# Good Knight!